"All of the sky is in the grass
and can be seen upside down."

Louis Aragon

Raphaël Thierry

Green Butterfly

a superdog adventure

Handprint Books
Brooklyn, New York

"Oh! You're all tied up!"

"It doesn't bother me much."

"Yes, but look at me . . .

I'm as free as a bird . . .

. . . and I can see everything upside down!"

But superdog is clever.

He too can see everything . . .

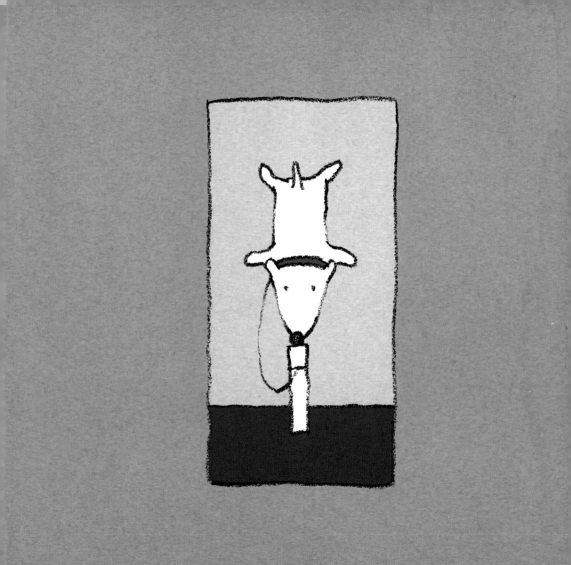

. . . upside down!

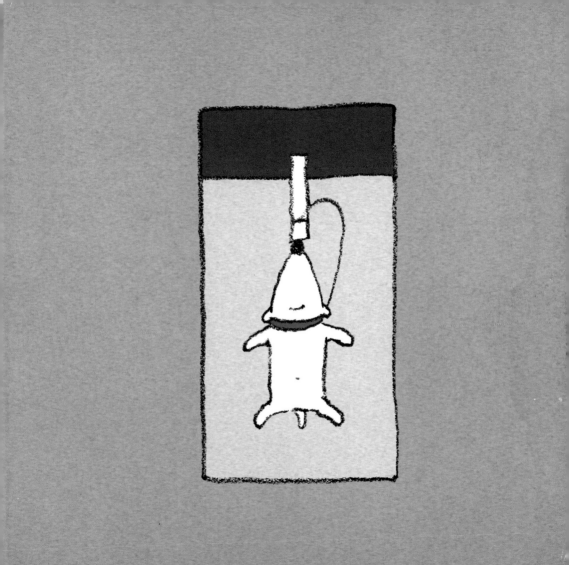

Well, almost everything.

First published in the United States in 2007
by Handprint Books Inc.
413 Sixth Avenue, Brooklyn, NY 11215
www.handprintbooks.com
Originally published in 2000 by Éditions Magnard
under the title: Papillon Vert - une aventure de Superchien
First English-language edition published 2005 by
Andersen Press Ltd., London
This edition published by arrangement with Andersen Press Ltd.
Copyright © Éditions Magnard, 2000 - Paris
English translation © 2005 by Raphaël Thierry and Jeffrey Paul Kearney
All rights reserved.
Printed and bound in China.

ISBN 13: 978-1-59354-198-9
ISBN 10: 1-59354-198-8
2 4 6 8 10 9 7 5 3 1